KARATE KIDS

Cody
THE
Tang Soo
Dodo

TIES HIS SHOES

WRITTEN BY SEAN KINNEY
ILLUSTRATED BY MELISSA KINNEY

"Cody!" Mama Dodo called one Monday afternoon. "It's time for karate class. Come on, put on your shoes!"

Cody, already wearing his gi and belt, was flitting about his room in a tizzy.

"Mom, I can't find my boots. I've looked everywhere!"

Cody was searching in all the usual places - on the shelf in his closet, in the mudroom cubby, on top of his dresser, in his school backpack, behind his bedroom door, behind the curtains...he even checked under his covers in case he had forgotten to take them off before bed and kicked them off in his sleep, but nope.

THEY WERE GONE!

"Well grab your sneakers then, honey, and let's go!" his mom called back.

Gulp Cody kept looking. Cody did not want his sneakers. He just knew that if he had to wear his sneakers, his mom was going to make him try to tie them himself.

He looked in the corner. There they were: his orange and grey striped sneakers. He loved orange.

Practically everything he owns is orange. He even loves oranges and orange soda. And he was soooooo thrilled when he earned his orange Tang Soo Do belt! But Cody didn't like his orange sneakers.

He slumped and walked over to them.
He picked them up.
He looked them over.

Hmmmm, he said to himself.

"I'll be right out!" he called back to his mother.

He woefully looked around the room one last time...no boots.

He sat on his toy box and slipped on his untied sneakers. Cody may have been right handed, but Master Mantis told him he was left footed. He started with the left one.

The ends of the shoelace dangled down on either side of the shoe. He picked them up and gave it a try...

Cross them, and tuck one under? Um, no, wait...how do I do the bunny ears?...

Cody struggled for a minute and when he was done, his shoe had fallen off his foot, he had slipped off the toy box onto the floor, and had practically tied his wings together with the laces.

Cody started to cry.

"Mom, I can't do it," he wailed. "I can't find my boots and I can't tie my sneakers. Can I just stay home?"

He pouted.

Mama Dodo came around the corner and into his room.

"Oh Cody, don't cry!" she said, wiping his tears. She slipped his shoe back on his foot. "You just need practice, that's all!"

Cody looked down; he didn't want to practice.

"Let's not be late for class," his mom said. "We can work on them later on tonight."

Cody watched as   *ZIP! ZIP! ZIP!*

his mom tied his shoe in an instant. She reached over and tied the second one.

ZIP! ZIP! ZIP!

He wiggled his feet and stood up. They were perfect - not too loose, not too tight. They were just right!

He beamed. Cody flapped his wings, and took off into a flying side kick. "Hi-ya!" he shouted, as he landed and ran down the hall to the door. "Let's go!"

Cody and his mom arrived at the Do Jang, the studio where he practices Tang Soo Do, a form of martial arts.

He walked into the studio quietly and in control of his body, just like a Tang Soo Do warrior. That was hard!

Cody slipped off his shoes and slid them into a locker. He made sure not to let the ties come undone so he wouldn't have to try to tie them on his way out. Then he stood in the corner of the Do Jang, bowed in respect and sat on the mat, his legs crossed like a pretzel, and waited for class to begin.

Class always started with an opening routine and he bowed to his instructor, paid respect to the country's flag, and recited the students' creed. Tonight, while he shouted the creed with all his classmates, one phrase stuck in his head: "Don't say, 'I can't.'"

He continued reciting the rest of the creed, but in his mind, he was repeating,

Don't say, "I can't."
Don't say, 'I can't."

Never give up, he thought to himself.

In class, Cody practiced all of his moves.

He completed his star block set.
That was fun and easy, but he had to
perform it in a horse stance - a GREAT
horse stance. That was hard, too, but in
his head, Cody kept repeating,
Don't say, "I can't."

They practiced
their punches
and kicks,
their front stance,
and their cat
stance.

"Don't say,
'I can't,'" he heard
Master Mantis'
voice in his head.

He shouted
"Hi-ya!" loud
and proud with
every move.

He felt *AWESOME*.

His moves were so fast and strong that the knot in his belt became loose...

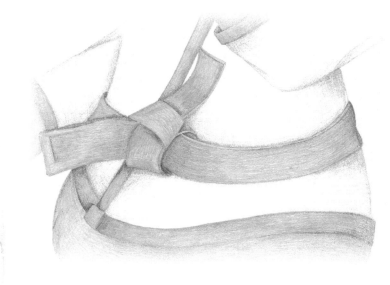

and then looser...

and then looser.

Cody wasn't paying attention to his belt. He was doing his best to pay attention to Master Mantis, and his belt began to slowly unravel. Cody didn't even notice. He just stayed focused on listening to the instructor shouting commands.

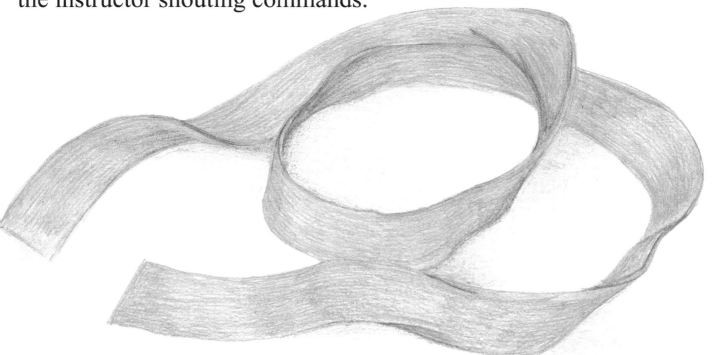

While he and his classmates finished a tough set of front kicks in a strong guard stance, Master Mantis was making his way around the group, providing direction where needed. He stopped at Cody, looked down and saw that Cody's belt had slipped all the way off and was laying on the floor.

Master Mantis smiled.

"CODDYYYY," he cried cheerily, "Your kicks are so awesome that your belt is trying to run away!"

The class burst out laughing.

Master Mantis bent down and swooped up the belt from the floor. And just like his mom had done with his shoes,
ZIP! ZIP! ZIP!
In a flash of movement, Master Mantis had thrown the belt around Cody's waist and created the tightest knot Cody had ever seen in his belt.

"Now that you're an orange belt, I suppose you should be tying this on your own!" Master Mantis said.

Cody's face flushed. His head began to spin.

Tie my shoes AND tie my belt?! BUT I CAN'T, he thought. Cody tried to do his best, but now his kicks seemed a bit halfhearted. He wasn't as excited as he had been when he first arrived. He was feeling a little mad at belts and at laces, and at teachers, and at moms.

Cody bowed on his way out of class, but not the way he did on his way in. His shoulders slumped, his smile now a frown, and he sulked his way to the locker to grab his shoes.

He grabbed each sneaker, one at a time, and wiggled, shook, slammed, and crammed, and fought to squeeze his feet into his already-tied shoes.

Cody felt upset.
On the car ride home,
he stayed quiet.

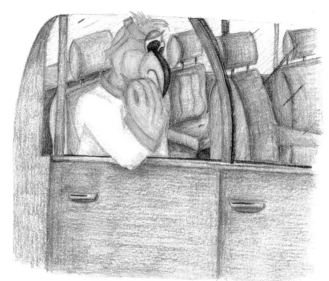

When he ate dinner,
he stayed quiet.

When he got ready for bed,
he stayed quiet.

When he climbed in bed and closed his eyes, he made himself a promise.

I'm going to learn to tie my shoes and to tie my belt. Don't say, "I Can't."

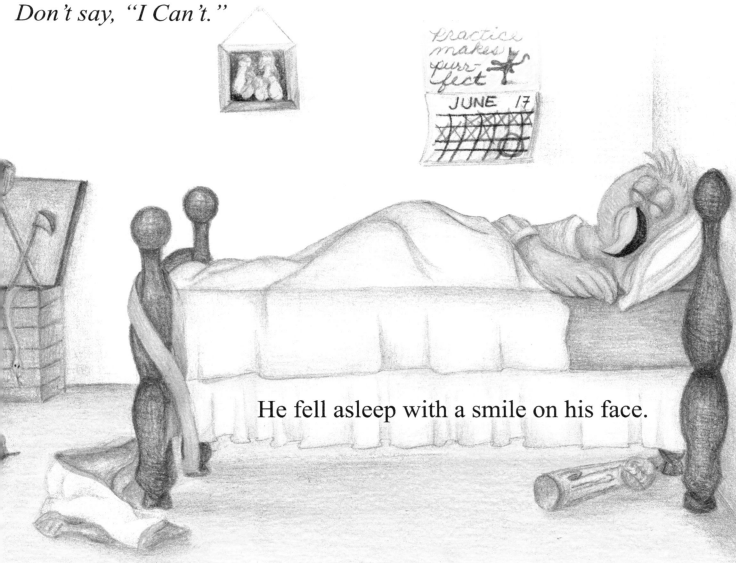

He fell asleep with a smile on his face.

The next morning, Cody woke up early.

He was going to need extra time if he was going to tie his shoes.

Cody got dressed, then he sat on his toy box and slipped on his sneakers.

The ends of the shoe lace dangled down on either side of the shoe. He grabbed them up and gave it a try.

Ok, cross them, and tuck one under? That's not working.
What if I...no, wait....

When Cody was done, his shoe had fallen off his foot, he had slipped off the toy box onto the floor, and he had practically tied his wings together with the laces.

But this time, he didn't panic. This time he didn't cry.

"Don't say, 'I can't,'" he stated.

"Hey, Mom!" he called, "what's the rhyme about how to do my laces again?"

His mom came around the corner, leaned against the doorway and sung,

Over and under, and pull it tight.
Make a bow and pull it through
to tie it right!

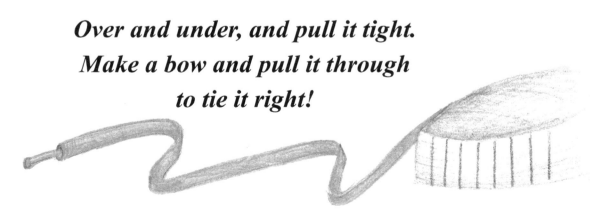

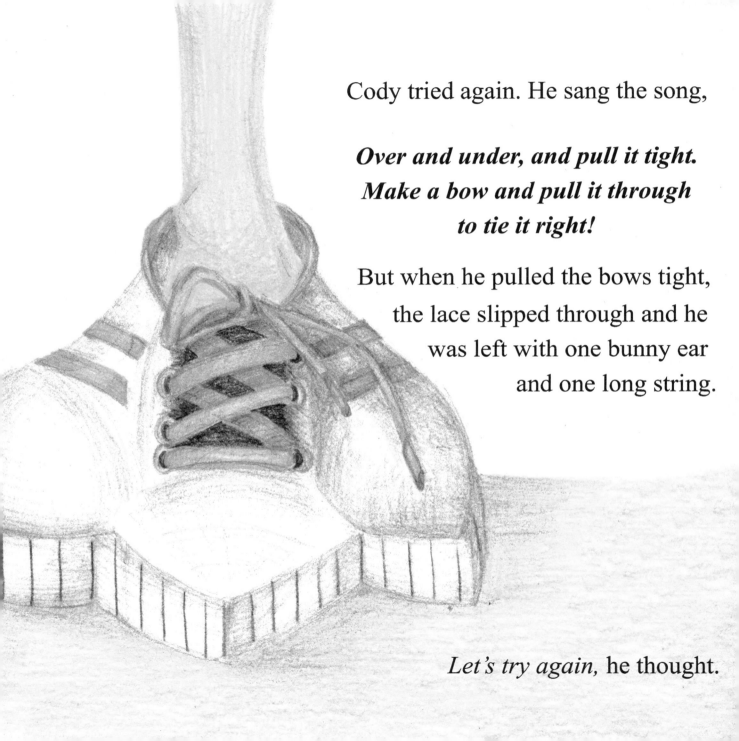

Cody tried again. He sang the song,

Over and under, and pull it tight.
Make a bow and pull it through
to tie it right!

But when he pulled the bows tight,
the lace slipped through and he
was left with one bunny ear
and one long string.

Let's try again, he thought.

And he did, but this time the other bunny ear fell out. And again...and again...and again.

Cody tried seven times, and each time, something went wrong. By the end, he was crying again.

"I can't do it!" he wailed.

Mom wiped his tears.

"No, Cody, you can't do it YET! You just need to keep trying. You'll get there."

Cody wore his boots to school on Tuesday.

After school, Cody went in his room, quietly shut the door, and stayed alone for almost half an hour. His mom walked by several times to listen in. All she heard was humming.

And so it went on for the next two days. Every night, Cody went to bed and made his promise, and every morning he tried and tried, but still couldn't tie his shoes.

He cried and sniffled.

He wore his Crocs to school on Wednesday, his flip-flops on Thursday, and his rain boots on Friday.

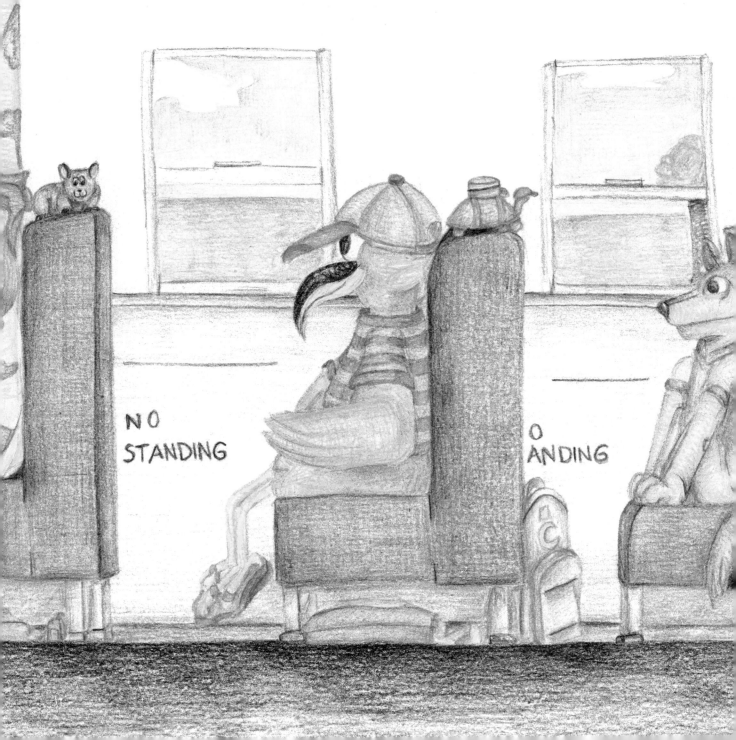

Each afternoon, Cody
went into his room and
quietly shut the door.
His mom walked by
several times to listen in,
but all she could heard
was humming.

He practiced all day
Saturday and Sunday, and
on these days, he didn't
cry - only sniffled.

"I'll do it, Mom. I just can't do it YET!!"

Sunday night, Cody checked his alarm clock. He said his promise and he went to sleep with a smile.

On Monday morning, Cody woke up, got dressed, sat on his toy box and slipped on his sneakers. He started with the left one.

The ends of the shoe lace dangled down on either side of the shoe.

Cody pulled the laces through and pulled them tight.

He looked down. His shoe was tied.

It wasn't too loose, it wasn't too tight. It was just right.

Cody moved onto the right shoe.

He pulled the laces through and gave them a tug.
He looked down. Now THAT shoe was tied.

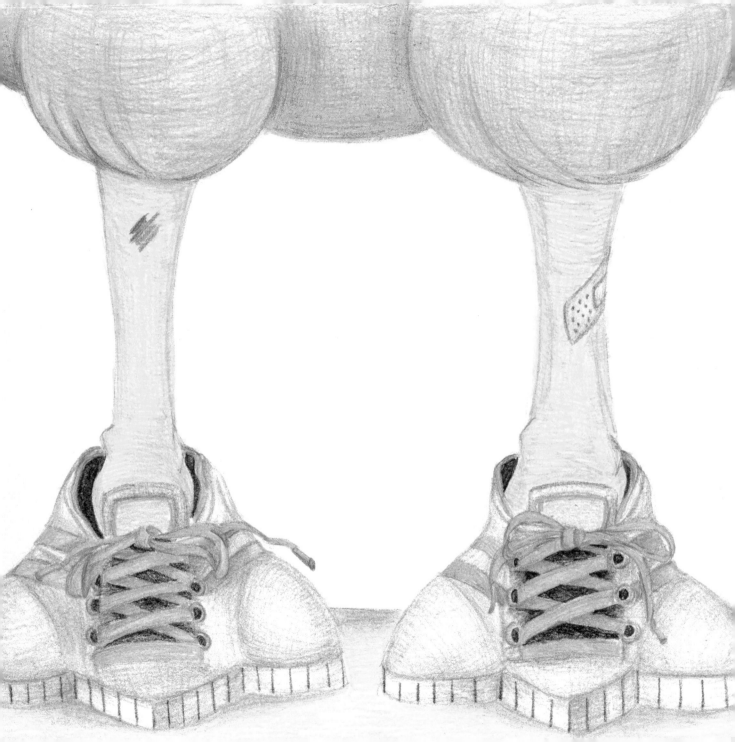

Cody wore his sneakers all day. He told EVERYONE that he had tied them himself. EVERYONE.

He ran out of the room and told the dog.

He told his sisters who were eating pancakes with syrup (Cody LOVED pancakes with syrup).

Cody told his dad as he was leaving for work.

He told the
bus driver,

his classmates,

his teachers,

the principal,

the lunch ladies,

and on his way home,
he told the bus driver
again, just to make
sure she remembered.

After school, Cody changed into his gi and played in his room.

"Cody!" his mom called, "It's almost time to leave for karate. Let's go - put on your shoes!"

"They're already on!" he beamed, running into the kitchen with his karate belt, "and watch THIS!"

Cody grabbed his belt and went to work...singing a new song as he went.

Hold the left end, wrap it twice,
right end goes under, pull it nice,

(Cody watched his hands and scrunched his eyes.)

then right over left and pull it through…

(Cody's tongue stuck out of his mouth as he concentrated really hard.)

then snap it tight is all you've got to do!

"Wow, Cody!" Mom exclaimed, "You never quit and now you can tie your shoes AND your belt!"

Cody looked up, snapping his belt ends tight a couple times.

"Wait until Master Mantis sees this!!" He exclaimed.

His mom grinned. "So THAT'S what you've been up to, cooped up in your room all week."

When Cody got to class, he walked in quietly and in control of his body, (that was STILL hard), pulled off his shoes, and slid them into a locker.

He didn't care that they had come undone. He could tie them! Then he stood in the corner of the Do Jang, bowed in respect and sat on the floor, legs crossed like a pretzel and waited for class to begin.

Just like last Monday's class, he felt *AWESOME*. Punches and kicks, front stances, cat stances...he shouted "Hi-Ya!" loud and proud with every move.

He did his best, and his moves again were so fast and strong that the knot in his belt became loose...and looser...and looser. And just like last Monday, Cody didn't notice. He was focused on listening to the instructions.

While he and his classmates finished a tough set frog jumps, Master Mantis was making his way around the group, helping other students. He stopped at Cody, looked down and saw that Cody's belt had slipped all the way off and was laying on the floor again.

Master Mantis smiled. "CODDDYYYYY" he cried cheerily, "Your frog jumps are so high that your belt can't keep up!"

The class burst out laughing.

This time, Cody swooped up his belt from the floor, he held the left end in one hand and the right end in the other. He whispered his song....

> *Hold the left end, wrap it twice,*
> *right end goes under, pull it nice,*
> *then right over left and pull it through...*
> *then snap it tight is all you've got to do!*

Cody snapped his belt ends and looked up.

"Wow!" said Master Mantis with a smile. "Now that you're an orange belt I suppose you CAN tie it on your own!!"

Master Mantis patted him on the back and walked back up to the front of the class.

Never give up,
Cody thought.

Beaming with pride, he
pumped his fist in the
air and yelled,

"Don't say, 'I Can't!'
TANG SOO!"

Think Like a Martial Artist!

Start up some great conversation between you and your child!

Winners Never Quit

- Cody spent a long time practicing tying both his shoes and his belt. What are some skills that you have practiced again and again to master? What are some things you are still practicing?

- There were times in the story where Cody still hadn't mastered tying his sneakers. He was going to take some time to practice, but he also still needed to wear something on his feet to school each day. How did he find ways to solve his problem while he continued to learn to tie his shoes?

- What was the strategy Cody used to to help him remember how to work with his shoelaces? Have you ever used special strategies to learn something challenging?

- In the end of the story, how did Cody feel? How do you know? How did you feel when you mastered something new?